CW00855422

with Love and best wishes
this day forward xx

WHAT A LOVELY STORY

says PAUL CHUCKLE of the Legendary Chuckle Brothers

I once thought I would like to be a ballet dancer but I kept tripping myself up! Even a mouse could dance better than me – especially a very talented young lady mouse called Pearl.

I loved reading this story and I hope there will be many more……

Pearl Pavlova

Annie Day Fernie

Illustated by
Lizzie Birney

2021

PEARL PAVLOVA
BY ANNIE DAY FERNIE

 ILLUSTRATIONS BY
Lizzie B ILLUSTRATION

EDITED BY MICA BALE

Published by MIGHTY PENS LTD
mightypens.co.uk

ISBN: 978-1-8382882-1-1

Page design: Pageset Ltd
Printed by Ridgeway Press, Breach House, Easton Royal Pewsey Wiltshire SN9 5LU

Prepared by Mighty Pens Ltd.
mightypens.co.uk

For
Mamushka Mariya

Walk Tall, Walk Bravely

Introducing...

Rostislav

Freddi

Piotr

Katrina

Pearl

Niki

Also featuring: Anna, Madame Mousska & Madame Nina

"**Oh** Katrina, she is so beautiful," Anna looked at the little pup lying in her mother's arms. She was pink with just the first hint of lustrous white fur. She looked like a beautiful pearl and Anna said so.

"Anna, that would be the perfect name for her," said Katrina. "Pearl it is!" Katrina's eyes filled with tears. "I wish her Papa were here to see her…"

It was a bleak day in St. Petersburg at the Mariinsky Theatre but Madame Mousska of the Mousska Ballet was adamant that her little students should come to class despite the chilliness of the studio underneath the stage where they practised. Little mice without a care. They did work hard but perhaps some less than others. Their tiny shoes were left discarded when too old or out of shape, ready for someone else to pick up.

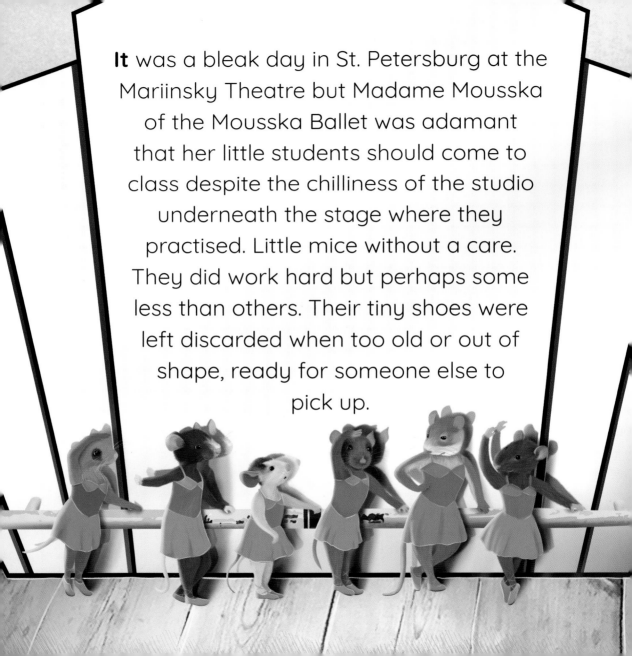

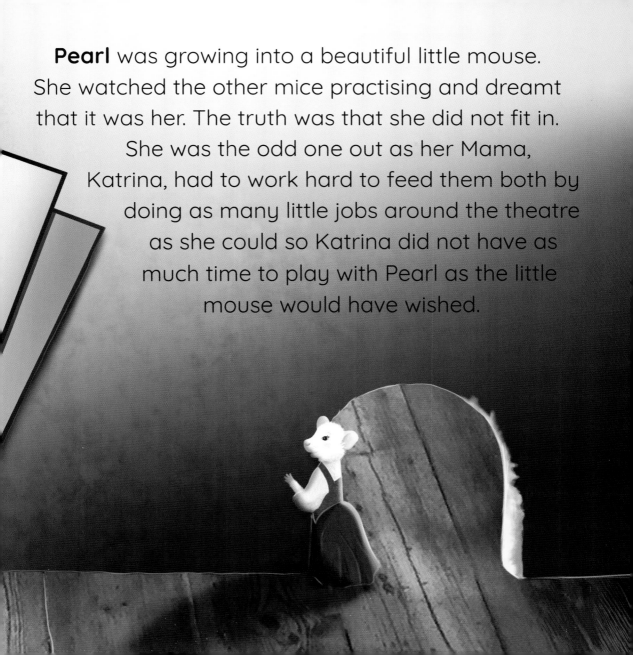

Pearl was growing into a beautiful little mouse.
She watched the other mice practising and dreamt
that it was her. The truth was that she did not fit in.
She was the odd one out as her Mama,
Katrina, had to work hard to feed them both by
doing as many little jobs around the theatre
as she could so Katrina did not have as
much time to play with Pearl as the little
mouse would have wished.

When Pearl wasn't helping her Mama she would watch the classes and try to copy the moves they made. They were complicated but she had a quick mind and an able, supple body.
Pearl soon mastered the steps and realised that the discarded old ballet shoes were just that. She took a little pair of the well-worn, satin pumps and tried them on. They were a little ill-fitting but made her feel as though she could really dance.

One day when Pearl was practising, Madame Mousska happened to see her. She was charmed. Pearl moved with skill and looked beautiful. It was clear she had had no formal training but she was a natural.

Madame spoke to her. Poor Pearl got a fright and thought she was to get a row but no, Madame spoke gently to her. "My child, what is your name?"

"Pearl – Madame!" Pearl answered clearly.

"Would you like me to help you perfect the movements you are making?" Madame asked kindly. Pearl's eyes shone. "Yes please Madame." And so Madame would give her a little lesson every day.

Pearl's life was not easy. She was an only pup with no brothers or sisters to play with or help with the chores in the poor but clean mouse hole where they lived. Pearl did not know her Papa. She knew that he had been taken away by Rostislav, a large, black, angry rat who, like her Papa, had never been seen since. It was hard for her Mama to bear that she would never see her beloved husband again.

The Mariinsky Theatre in St. Petersburg is a beautiful old building and houses both the Mariinsky Opera and the Mariinsky Ballet. As with all theatres, it has its own special magic and is home to many creatures.

The theatre has strange traditions and is even haunted by those who have danced and sung there in the past!

The mice population is large, as you might imagine, but it is one special mouse that we are going to talk about now...

Frederick! Freddi to his friends. Freddi had seen Pearl dancing and had fallen in love with her. He wanted to be her friend and take care of her. He just needed to introduce himself!!

"**Hrmph!**" Freddi coughed.
No response! "Hrmph, Hrmph!!"
Pearl turned round to see a little brown
mouse with sparkling eyes and finally realised
he was trying to attract her attention.
"Oh hello!" Pearl said, "I didn't see you there.
Sorry!"
"Oh don't worry. I am just being nosey. You are
a lovely dancer!" Freddi said. "Are you in the
Ballet Company?"
"Me?" said Pearl, with surprise. "No! I could never
be in the Company."
"Oh, I think you could," said Freddi, with a
twinkle in his eye.

Freddi and Pearl became fast friends. When they weren't helping at home and Pearl wasn't practising, they would play tag in the orchestra pit until they heard the musicians arriving for rehearsal or a matinee. They didn't dare play there between the Matinee and the Evening Performance. They had great fun and Pearl started to confide in Freddi about her Papa.

"And Papa was never seen again..." Pearl started sobbing as though her little mouse heart was breaking! She had just finished describing how her Papa had discovered a thief taking items from the local community of mouse holes. Her Papa had come upon the thief on his nightly round. The perpetrator had grabbed Papa and ran off into the shadows with him!

"Oh Freddi. He was a huge black RAT! He is known as Rostislav and...and...and..." Pearl burst into a fresh bout of tears which streamed down her fur like little sparkling diamonds. In spite of that she looked even more beautiful to Freddi.

Freddi tried hard to comfort Pearl. He took her tiny paw and rubbed the palm of it.

"What is your Papa's name?" He said.

"Nikolai or Niki for short," Pearl answered with a sniff.

"Ah! That makes sense!" said Freddi.

"Does it?" said Pearl.

"Yes!" said Freddi, emphatically. Pearl waited as he went on.

"Nikolai means Victor of the People," Freddi explained. "That tells me that your Papa is a strong mouse and where there is strength there is hope!"

Freddi saw a light flickering in Pearl's eyes and her tears started to dry.

Items had started to go missing from the mouse holes again. Anna came to Katrina and Pearl's home to tell them. Katrina looked worried and scared. She felt it could only mean one thing, Rostislav was becoming brave again. She was frightened of what that would mean for herself and Pearl.

Katrina had seen how settled and happy Pearl had been recently. She did not want that spoiled for her lovely little pup. She looked like an angel and danced like a dream. Katrina bent her head deep in thought.

Freddi looked at the note in his paw that had been left at the door of his mouse hole. He was puzzled. Who would want to write to him? Maybe it was Pearl cancelling their arrangement to meet behind the percussion section of the orchestra? He sighed!

Opening the envelope he saw that the letter was from Pearl's Mama. It looked like it had been written hastily. He read it several times and wondered how he could achieve what she asked. He strode up and down the floor nibbling absently on a piece of cheese then stopped short.

"I know exactly what to do!"

Meanwhile, Katrina was tearfully packing a small bag for Pearl. In it she put her favourite things and in particular her little satin ballet shoes.

She also put in the locket that had come from her own Mama which contained a lock of fur the same colour as Pearl's. Katrina hoped it would keep her darling safe. She had to trust Freddi. He was a fine young pup with a good head on his shoulders.

The network of mice messengers throughout all the theatres in the world would hopefully keep her informed and there was a place that Freddi knew Pearl would be very safe.

"We, my dearest Pearl," Freddi said, "Are going to London to make you a famous mouse ballerina. You have so much talent let us not waste it here where the other mice will make it difficult for you. They are jealous!" And so, with their bags packed and Mama's blessing, Pearl and Freddi embarked on the long journey to St. Petersburg's seaport to catch the ocean liner that would then take them to the port of Southampton which served the City of London.
They would be cared for by the other ocean liner mice as they made the journey across the grand Baltic Sea.

Nor

De

North Sea

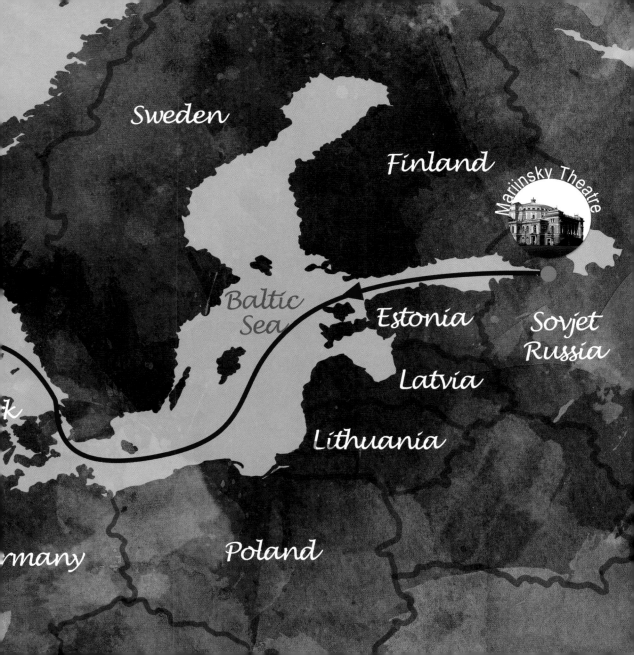

Sweden

Finland

Mariinsky Theatre

Baltic
Sea

Estonia

Sovjet
Russia

Latvia

Lithuania

Poland

many

The first part of the journey was by an old fashioned steam train and then there was a long walk before they were safely ushered onto the liner by their new friends. They were shown to two tiny but clean mouse holes behind the kitchen of the enormous ship. They were even shown how to secure the tiny life jackets in the unlikely event that the ship ran into problems. Then, with a big blast of the ship's horn, the huge liner was on its way with an enormous plume of smoke trailing behind it.

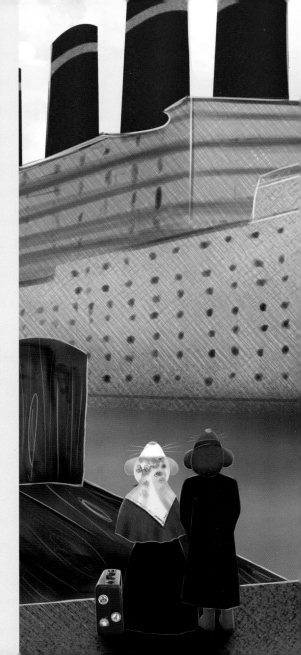

Pearl was a little seasick at the beginning but gradually settled down. Some ginger and hot water settled her stomach and soon she was enjoying the movement of the ship and the wind blowing in her face when they could get out of their tiny mouse hole cabins.
They had to be careful as there were many people on the ship and they constantly walked up and down the deck but early morning and late evening offered some freedom
But Pearl was to discover a wonderful thing about ocean liners!

"**Oh** Freddi, there is a ballet studio here!" She said.

As in the Mariinsky Theatre, there was also a company of mouse dancers and when she was introduced to them she was warmly welcomed.

These were travelling dancing mice and they were kind and invited her to join their daily classes which Pearl was thrilled to do.

Gradually she became very good at the different moves she was learning and the ballet mistress was delighted with her.

Freddi and Pearl watched from the wings every night at the lavish performances that were put on for the passengers. Some performances were ballet but there were also other types of dance, magic, comedy and singing.

All too soon they were at their destination – Southampton. Bustling, noisy and very smelly! Strange accents and an entirely different language.

But despite how different the mouse population was, they were warm and friendly and joked and laughed with Freddi and Pearl as they took them to their final destination – Covent Garden the home of Sadlers Wells Ballet!

The corresponding mouse company was the Ballet Regina and it was Pearl's dearest wish that she may be accepted there.

The mouse holes in the Theatre were tiny and cramped but the atmosphere was wonderful. The smell of the greasepaint and the dancers' resin for their shoes was intoxicating. Pearl loved it.

Freddi watched Pearl grow in confidence as she came on remarkably quickly. The style of ballet she was learning was a little different but Pearl took to it very quickly. She was a natural and Freddi's heart swelled with pride.

Freddi had been able to get a message to Katrina that they were well and both Anna and Katrina breathed a sigh of relief as they read the message in the light of Katrina's mouse-hole.

Meanwhile, the thieving from the mouse-holes continued and the mice population was worried. They knew who the culprit was. There were many clues but they refused to be bullied and so it was that they had a meeting where they talked and pondered and finally came up with a plan.

Madame Nina watched her newest pupil with great interest. She admired Pearl's delicate poise, her fluttering, graceful arms and her very Russian technique. The perfect turn out and flattened back.

The young mouse really was a wonderful homage to Pearl's namesake, the great Pavlova. Madame approached the delicate creature and welcomed her to class. Pearl inclined her beautiful head and thanked Madame for allowing her this wonderful opportunity.

The large mouse population had gathered in the mouse hall which was the largest space they could find. A plan was made to stop the thieving by Rostislav. Sentries were to be placed at each mouse hole, dressed in dark clothing so that their presence would not be detected.

When Rostislav appeared, as he was now doing nightly, a group of them would stealthily follow him to wherever he was going. It was likely that he would be going down into the depths of the City. In other words the sewers...

There was a rustle and then the scraping of what sounded like a cane against the stone floor. A wheezing sound accompanied the intruder. Rostislav! The sentries were silent. This was the rat that was used by their Mamas to frighten them when they were misbehaving young pups.

He looked old and broken down and what little light there was caught the silver in his previously ebony coat.

If Rostislav wondered why the mice had taken to leaving their food so close to the doors of their mouseholes he did not pursue that thought. He was hungry and ill.

At a nod from their commander, the chosen group of mice silently followed Rostislav. Down and down they went far below the lowest floors of the theatre. At last they arrived at the final destination with Rostislav just ahead of them. He almost collapsed outside a little hut-like structure. "Niki?" He wheezed, "I am back with food."

"I have the cheese you are so fond of and other delights. I will leave them here. I am not hungry tonight so take your fill!" Rostislav said before shuffling off.

Niki looked out the door of the hut and picked up the food. In the gloom he saw the bright eyes of several mice looking at them.

As his eyes became accustomed to the dark, he could see that they were the eyes of his friends and neighbours. At last he would be rescued. He was torn. He had become strangely fond of his captor!

The bold and brash Rostislav had softened as his health deteriorated. Too many years of living alone in the oppressive darkness of the sewers and eating the contaminated food floating in the water had taken a dreadful toll on him.

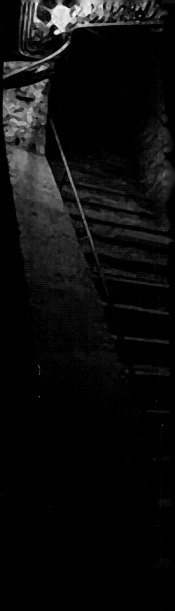

"Piotr, my friend," said Niki, peering through the darkness at the mouse, "I thought I should never see you again. I know it has only been months but it might as well have been centuries."

He paused before saying, "Rostislav is close to death. I fear that he may not survive the night. I was frightened at first but then I realised he was just a very lonely, bitter and frightened rat deserted by family and friends."

The other mice nodded and agreed that they should simply make the long journey back up to their homes, taking Niki with them of course.

"But I cannot just go without seeing him again!" Niki protested. "I need to see if he wants anything before I go!"
His friends and neighbours looked puzzled but shrugged their shoulders. They were just pleased to have found their friend safe and well.

Niki crept slowly towards his former captor. Rostislav looked at him warily. "Have they found you?" said Rostislav, "I knew that they were following me. You mice smell differently. They were clever and I could not see them but I felt their presence. I am sorry Niki. What I did was very wrong. Go and be happy with your little family. My time is near..." And with a flick of his paw Rostislav dismissed Niki.

"Can I get you anything?" Niki said.

"No Niki. I am comfortable enough, just weary," said Rostislav.

He turned his head away but not before Niki saw just the glimmer of a tear tracking its way down the fur of his cheek. With a sigh Niki said his final goodbyes.

Niki squared his shoulders and joined his friends as they scampered up the rocky and uneven floor of the underground cavern they had found themselves in.

"**Niki?**" said Katrina. She could hardly breathe. She knew of course what the mice had planned but she thought that it was simply not possible that her beloved was still alive.

Katrina had heard so many nasty stories about Rostislav but now was not the time for too many questions. This was a time for rejoicing and rejoice they did!

The lights were turned up. Platters of food were delivered from mouse-hole to mouse-hole but finally the mice population settled for the night and as Katrina held Niki close she whispered her plans for a long voyage.

And so it was that Katrina and Niki followed the
journey that Freddi and Pearl had made some time
previously. The same steam train, the same ocean
liner and finally the same smelly, busy Southampton
to meet the witty, charming cockney mice that
had escorted Freddi and Pearl to Covent Garden.
Accommodation was soon found for them.

On their first night in London they were presented with a feast of cheese fondue with thimblesful of ale to wash it down.

They rested well that night. Tomorrow night was to be one of great excitement for them both. There was to be a visit to a London theatre to see a very special little mouse!

Madame Nina embraced Pearl. "Now dance my child like you have never danced before!" She said. "This was created for the great Pavlova. You are no longer a mouse, you are an elegant swan!"

Madame Nina went on, "Remember Pearl you can be anything you choose to be in life but also remember what you do must be done for good and not for evil."

Pearl breathed in deeply and took position as the theatre lights dimmed and the curtain rose. The strains of the beautiful orchestra filled the theatre and Pearl was transcended to another world. She danced as if the stars were her stage.

The applause was thunderous! Pearl came out of her trance. Her debut was over. The audience were on their feet. She was a triumph!
She glanced down to the footlights and saw her beloved Mama with a handsome stranger sitting in the front row of the stalls.
At a nod from Madame she was permitted to go into the audience to embrace her Mama. She looked at the stranger and then her Mama with a puzzled look on her face. Her Mama nodded, "Yes your Papa has returned to us."
Pearl was swept into his very loving arms. This stranger was her adored Papa and her heart had never been more full.

EPILOGUE

"**Freddi** you are a dark horse!" Pearl said, a smile breaking onto her face.

"Well actually I think you will find I am a mouse," Freddi grinned. "Horses! Pah! Large sweaty creatures!" He pretended to shudder then said.

"Okay, so I knew what was going to happen but it could all have gone wrong and we lost touch when the communication chain broke down and it wasn't certain..." Freddi trailed off.

"Freddi you are the most wonderful friend a girl could ever have," Pearl said, wrapping her arms around him. Freddi just blushed, shrugged his shoulders and said cheekily, "You are right. I am!"

Somewhere over the rainbow way up high there's a land that I heard of once in a lullaby
Somewhere over the rainbow skies are blue and the dreams that you dare to dream really do come tr
Some day I'll wish upon a star and wake up where the clouds are far behind me
Where troubles melt like lemon drops away above the chimney tops that's where you'll find me
Somewhere over the rainbow bluebirds fly. Birds fly over the rainbow.
Why then, oh why can't I?

Author **Annie Day Fernie** has always had a passion for dance. Her youth was spent in ballet class, rehearsal and enjoying the magical world of performance. With experience as a teacher, Annie is always looking for new ways to engage young talent in the magnificent world of ballet and was inspired to write the story of Pearl, the young mouse who just couldn't sit still in her imagination. Annie is currently capturing more of Pearl's latest adventures in her upcoming books.

A talented graphic designer and artist, illustrator **Lizzie Birney** is no stranger to the world of performance and it was her friendship and role as a long standing musician in Annie's ballet class that inspired and fired an exciting partnership that would ultimately bring Pearl to life and into the spotlight.

Ingredients

3 Egg yolks / 1 egg white
40g unsalted butter
265g (¾ cup) honey
450g (3 cups) plain flour
3 tsp baking powder
½ tsp ground cinnamon
½ tsp ground ginger
55g (¼ cup) caster sugar

Topping

Water
Icing sugar
Red food colouring
Sugar Pearls

Pearl Pavlova's Pryaniki

When Pearl has been practicing hard and is very tired, she has one of these delightful little biscuits as a pick me up.
They are easy to make, so why not try making them with your adult helper?

1

Separate 2 eggs and keep the yolks. (Discard the egg whites or use them for another recipe)

Whisk the 2 egg yolks with 1 whole egg in a bowl with butter and honey.

2

Sift flour, baking powder and spices into a bowl and combine.

Make a well in the centre, add egg mixture and gradually combine.

3

Cover and refrigerate for 1 hour.

Preheat oven to 180°C. Line 2 oven trays with baking paper.

4

Using damp hands, shape tablespoonfuls of mixture into 24 balls and place on the trays.

5

Flatten them slightly and bake, swapping the trays halfway, for 15 minutes or until cooked through and golden.

Transfer to a wire rack to cool.

6

Sift the icing sugar into a bowl and gradually add water until the icing becomes stiff. Add a drop of red food colouring to make them pink.

Decorate your cooled biscuits and don't forget to add the sugar pearls. They are Pearl's favourite!